THE GROCERY MOUSE

THE GROCERY MOUSE

by *Eleanor Clymer*

WITH PICTURES BY JEANNE BENDICK

ROBERT M. MCBRIDE & COMPANY

1945

This book is dedicated to the little mouse in
his hole, the bird in the tree, the squirrel on
the branch, and all the other little wild animals
that live in the city.

CONTENTS

THE GROCERY MOUSE

CHAPTER 1

The Grocery Store

THE grocery store was all clean and white and shiny. There were new white counters, and clean pine shelves filled with cans and bottles, and boxes of crackers and cereal.

Everything was very tidy. You could see where everything was.

But there was one thing you couldn't see. In the back of the store, in a dark corner, was a little hole. It led to a warm, dark place under the floor. And that was where Squeaker lived with his mother and his father and his two brothers and two sisters.

Squeaker was a mouse.

In the daytime, the store was bright with sunshine and electric lights. It was full of people buying bread and apples and cheese and things. Then the mice slept in their holes under the floor.

But in the evening, after all the people had gone away,

the grocery man turned out the lights and went home to his supper. That was when the mice came out to find something to eat.

First the father mouse would come out. He would look all around to see that all was safe. Then he would go off about some important business.

Then the mother mouse would come out. She would look all around too. Then she would squeak, "All right, children. Come along."

Then the children scrambled out of the hole and raced up and down the floor.

While their mother was busy seeing what there was for dinner, the little mice played tag up and down the shelves. Patter, patter, their tiny feet raced around the counters.

Squeaker liked to hide in a dark corner and spring out at his sisters. They would squeak with fright, and Squeaker would laugh.

"Squeaker, stop that, you naughty mouse," his mother would say. "Come here, I've found a nice bit of cheese. And here's a cracker to go with it. Isn't it nice of that grocery man to sweep the floor in the morning instead of at night? But if you're not good you must go without your dinner. I shan't let you come out at night."

"Then may I come out in the daytime?" Squeaker asked.

"No, you may not," said his mother. "Mice never come out in the daytime. You mustn't say such naughty things."

Then Squeaker would seize the bit of cheese and dash off with it, while his brothers chased him. Or he would creep up behind one of his sisters and nip her with his little teeth, and then run away and laugh.

"I don't know what to do with that child," his mother said, shaking her head.

"He's just full of spirits," his father answered. "I used to be that way myself when I was young. He'll settle down some day."

"Yes, if he doesn't get caught first," said his mother.

So the mice ran about all night. Sometimes the moon shone through the big glass windows, and sometimes the lights of a car going by, late at night, flashed in on them. Then they frisked about, trying to catch their shadows. But when the sky grew light in the early morning, Mother and Father Mouse would squeak, "Time for bed, children," and all the little mice would scramble sleepily down their hole and curl up in their warm nest.

All but Squeaker. He was always the last one to go to bed. He wanted to stay up in the daytime. Sometimes his mother had to nip him to make him go to bed.

"I'm going to go out in the daytime some day," he whispered to his brothers. "See if I don't."

And one day he did. He waited till his family were all sound asleep. Very quietly he crept out of the nest and up through the hole. It was quite light in the store. People were walking about and talking. A lady pushed a little wagon full of packages right past him and nearly stepped on him.

Squeaker dashed across the floor, and hid behind some cracker boxes.

"Oh!" the lady cried. "I just saw a mouse!" And she pushed her wagon away as fast as she could.

"A mouse?" said the grocery man. "Well! I didn't know we had mice. Where did he go?"

And he walked all around, looking into the corners. But Squeaker stayed hidden behind the cracker boxes.

After a while he crept out and went very quietly along the wall. Not far away there was a little boy, eating animal crackers out of a box. Squeaker stopped and sniffed. The animal crackers smelled good. Suddenly the little boy pulled a lion out of the box and dropped it on the floor.

"I'll get that," said Squeaker to himself. He stole up to the lion, seized it in his teeth, and rushed to his hole.

He fell into the nest, still holding the lion. His mother woke up and looked at him.

"Squeaker!" she said. "Where have you been?"

Squeaker put down the cracker and said, "Oh, I just went out for a minute, and look what I found."

His mother was very cross with him. "You will get into trouble," she said. "Mice must not go out in the daytime. That is not the way for a mouse to behave."

Squeaker was quite surprised at himself. He knew very well that he had been naughty. But he was a little pleased with himself, too. However, he didn't want to be scolded any more. So he curled up and pretended to be asleep.

When his mother had gone back to sleep, he opened his eyes. His brothers and sisters were awake, looking at him. They were wondering how he had dared to go out all alone in the daytime.

"Weren't you scared?" one brother asked.

"No," said Squeaker. "It was fun. Want a piece of my cracker?"

Each of them had a bite. It was very good.

"Didn't anybody chase you?" his sister asked.

"Oh, pooh!" said Squeaker. "I can always run faster than those people. I guess if you're that big you can't go very fast. They have great big feet. You ought to see them."

"Well, you're supposed to sleep in the daytime," said his other sister. "A mouse should never do anything that all the other mice don't do."

"Well, I can't sleep in the daytime with all those people tramping around overhead," said Squeaker, "and I'm going to do it again."

CHAPTER 2

Cheese

So EVERY day when his family were asleep, Squeaker went out. And the more he did it, the smarter he felt.

"What a wonderful mouse I must be," he said to himself. "All the other mice have to stay in their holes, and I go out when I please."

Right in broad daylight, he would poke his little gray head out, look around with his little black eyes, and begin to nibble at a cracker box or a package of rice.

Scratch, scratch, went his little sharp teeth.

Sometimes the grocery man would hear him and say, "There's that mouse again."

And sometimes he would see him and run after him. Squeaker would whisk around and dash out of sight.

"I must get a cat," said the grocery man. "But I have never seen more than one mouse, so maybe I don't really need a cat. I'll think about it."

"Ha, ha," Squeaker laughed to himself. "He thinks there aren't any other mice. Wouldn't he be surprised if he came in after dark!"

Squeaker got braver and braver. One day he crept right up to the front of the counter. The grocery man was cutting cheese for an old lady.

"Half a pound, please," said the old lady, and the grocery man took his big knife and sliced off a piece.

My, that cheese smelled good. Squeaker sniffed so hard that his whiskers wiggled. He wished the man and the old lady would just go away and leave him alone with it. But they didn't. The grocery man put the big cheese back in the icebox. Squeaker could see it through the glass door. He hid in a corner and waited.

A little boy was the next customer. "My mother wants a quarter of a pound of butter," he said.

So the grocery man opened the icebox. He left the door open for a minute.

Whiz! went Squeaker into the icebox. He hid behind the big cheese and nibbled a bit. My, that cheese tasted good. He nibbled a bit more. And then bang! the door slammed shut.

Squeaker jumped. He gave a little squeak. But nothing happened. He nibbled some more.

But all of a sudden he began to shiver. It was cold in

that icebox. Squeaker peered around the side of the cheese. The door was shut tight. He couldn't get out.

He curled himself up in a ball. He tried to wrap his tail around himself, but he got colder and colder.

At last he got so cold that he ran right up to the glass door and gave a loud "Squeeek!"

"Look!" shouted the little boy. "There's a mouse in there!"

"A mouse!" cried the old lady.

"A mouse!" said the grocer, and he opened the door and tried to grab Squeaker. But Squeaker was too fast for him. Quick as a flash he dashed out and ran for his hole.

After him the little boy galloped, the old lady waddled, and the grocery man clumped. But they were too slow.

Pop! Squeaker was down the mousehole.

His mother woke up with a start. "What's the matter with you?" she said.

"I'm cold," he shivered. And he curled up close to his mother.

"I smell cheese," she said. "Where have you been?"

"Oh, Mother," said Squeaker, "there's a big cold place where they keep the cheese, and I got in there, and couldn't get out, and then they tried to catch me, but I got away. But I was so cold that I almost couldn't run."

"Well, curl up and get warm," said his mother. "It

would have served you right if they had caught you, you bad mouse. I guess now you'll mind what I say."

"Yes, Mother," said Squeaker. And he shut his eyes tight and went to sleep.

Up in the store the grocery man was saying, "I really must get a cat. I can't have that mouse frightening my best customers. And who knows, maybe there are more mice! Yes, I will get a cat. Even if she doesn't really catch the mice, at least she will scare them away."

CHAPTER 3

Saltina

THAT night Squeaker was so sleepy that when the other mice woke up and went out, he just couldn't get up. He curled up all by himself in the nest and went back to sleep. He was having a beautiful dream about a great big cheese with a hole in the middle and himself in the middle of the hole, eating his way out.

All of a sudden he heard a squeak. He woke up and looked around. There was a little mouse whom he had never seen before. She looked very scared. Squeaker thought she was the prettiest mouse he had ever seen. She had the smoothest fur and the brightest eyes and the longest tail.

"Hello," said Squeaker.

"Hello," said the little mouse. "Who are you? Where am I?"

"I'm Squeaker," said Squeaker. "This is our house. My mother is out. What's your name?"

"Saltina," said the little mouse.

"What a nice name," said Squeaker.

"Yes, isn't it?" said Saltina. "My mother called me that because I was born in a cracker box."

"Where did you come from?" Squeaker asked.

"We just moved into this store," said Saltina. "I was looking for our hole and I fell in here by mistake."

"Where's your mother?" Squeaker asked.

"Oh, she's busy getting stuff for a bed," said Saltina. "She told me to sit and wait for her, but I got tired of it. I wanted to explore."

"I like to explore too," said Squeaker.

"In the other store," said Saltina, "where we used to live, there were lots of places to explore. Old corners full of boxes and barrels, and shelves full of packages that nobody ever touched."

"Why did you move?" Squeaker asked.

"Somebody came and took all the things away and went out and locked the door. After that nobody came there, and there wasn't much to eat. So we squeezed through a crack and moved here. But this store is awfully clean, isn't it?"

"Oh, it's all right," said Squeaker. "I have a lot of fun, myself. I've been going out in the daytime. I get lots to eat that way."

"That must be fun," said Saltina.

"Yes, it is," said Squeaker. "You can go with me tomor-

row if you like. Will your mother mind?"

"Oh, I don't think so," said Saltina. "She says we're almost old enough to take care of ourselves."

"All right," said Squeaker. "I'll come to your house and call you. Where is your house?"

"It's in a corner near a stack of paper towels and soap," said Saltina. "Do you think you can find it?"

"Oh, yes," Squeaker said. "I know where that is."

Next morning, as soon as Squeaker heard people walking about overhead, he jumped out of the nest, ran to Saltina's house and said, "Eek! Come on out!"

Out popped Saltina. "Hello," she said. "I was waiting for you."

"Come on," said Squeaker. "I'll show you where the best places are." He scampered off to the cracker boxes. There were sure to be some crumbs there.

"This is fun," said Saltina, as she nibbled at a gingersnap.

Suddenly she stopped nibbling and sat very still.

"What's the matter?" Squeaker asked. "Come over here. I've found another piece."

"Sh!" said Saltina. "There's a cat."

Squeaker looked around. Sure enough, not far away was a furry black thing with green eyes. It was only a kitten, but Squeaker didn't know that. It was ever so much bigger than he was.

"Eek!" he squeaked.

The kitten was playing with a walnut that somebody had dropped. She was rolling it around like a ball.

When she heard Squeaker's scared little "Eek!" she sat up and looked around. Her short tail twitched. She crouched in a funny baby crouch, getting ready to jump.

"Hurry up!" cried Saltina. She began to run. Squeaker ran too, and the kitten ran after them. They ran all around the store. They streaked past the counter.

"Where are you going, kitty?" the grocery man exclaimed, leaning over the counter. "Well, I declare! She's after a mouse! I thought she was too young to hunt. Maybe we'll get rid of that pesky mouse."

He still thought there was only one mouse.

Squeaker and Saltina dashed behind a case of milk bottles and sat down to catch their breath.

The kitten looked around for them, but she couldn't find them. If she had been a big old cat she would have hunted for them, and waited till they came out. But she was only a baby. She soon forgot about the mice and sat down to wash her paws.

Squeaker and Saltina sat very still in their hiding place. They sat there for a long time.

At last Squeaker said, "Do you think we can come out now?"

"I'll look," said Saltina, creeping to the edge of the box.

"Wait, let me look," Squeaker whispered.

"No, I will," said Saltina. "I know about cats. They had one in the other store I lived in."

She put her head out and wiggled her whiskers. Then she said, "Come on, I think we can get home. The cat is taking a nap."

The two mice stole out quietly and crept along the wall. Nobody saw them. Right ahead of them was a lady reaching up to a shelf for a can of peaches. She was right in Saltina's way and Saltina ran over her foot. The lady looked down, gave a screech, and dropped the can of peaches. It almost fell on Squeaker. Squeaker said "Eek!" and galloped over the lady's other foot.

"Help!" cried the lady. "One mouse ran over my foot, and then another mouse ran over my other foot!"

The two mice ran for their lives. But now people came from everywhere. The kitten woke up and came too.

Around and around they chased the two mice.

"Here they are!" screamed a little girl, and everybody ran with her.

"No, they're over here," a boy shouted. And everybody ran that way.

Away ran Saltina and Squeaker, right for the open door, and out into the street. Bang! went the door.

"Well!" the grocery man was saying, inside the door. "We didn't catch them, but at least we got them out." And he went back to his counter.

The lady whose feet the mice had run over had to sit down and rest. She fanned herself with a handkerchief.

"That gave me quite a turn," she said in a weak voice.

Down under the floor, in their nests, the mouse families were awake.

"What do you suppose all that commotion was about?" Squeaker's mother wondered. "Where is Squeaker?"

"He's gone," said the little mice.

"Well, I do hope nothing has happened to him," said his mother. "I warned him. But he wouldn't listen."

"He'll settle down some day," said his father. "He'll be back. I was just like that myself when I was young, and look at me now."

And he turned over and went back to sleep. All the other mice went to sleep too. Mice are not much given to worrying.

As for Saltina's mother, she didn't even wake up. She was too tired from moving.

CHAPTER 4

An Exciting Trip

OUT in the street, Squeaker and Saltina crouched close to the brick wall and wondered what to do.

"Shall we wait till somebody opens the door and go back in?" said Squeaker.

"No," said Saltina. "They might be watching for us. They might even set a trap."

"What's that?" Squeaker asked.

"Oh, it's a terrible thing," said Saltina. "I don't know what it is exactly, but I've heard my mother talk about it. My uncle was caught in a trap once."

"What happened to him?" Squeaker asked.

"I don't know," said Saltina. "I never saw him again. But I think we'd better find some other place to live."

Piled up against the wall of the store were some big wooden boxes. They were the boxes in which the bread was brought to the store. There was a nice smell of bread crumbs about them. Squeaker climbed over the edge of one of the big boxes and popped down inside.

"Come on in," he cried to Saltina. "It's nice in here."

Saltina climbed up and looked in. "It smells nice," she said, "but is there anything to eat?"

"Yes," said Squeaker. "Crumbs."

Saltina jumped down and ate some crumbs. "These are good," she said. "I like it in here. But my, isn't it hot!"

She looked up. The sun was shining right down into the box. Saltina had never seen the sun before. She didn't know what it was. She went over to a shady corner of the box and sat down.

"I wonder what will happen next," said Squeaker.

What happened next was that a bread truck drove up and stopped in front of the store. The driver jumped down and picked up the box they were sitting in and swung it up

on the back of the truck. Then he picked up the other boxes and piled them on top. Then he jumped into his seat and drove off.

Squeaker and Saltina rattled around in the box as the truck swung and swayed around a corner.

"Whee!" said Squeaker, running around in the box. "What kind of place is this?"

"I—I don't know," gasped Saltina. "I can't get my breath. Oh, dear! Why did we ever get in here? Maybe this is a trap."

"No, I don't think so," said Squeaker. "I don't see how to get out, but maybe something else will happen."

"Everything is happening today," said Saltina.

Something did happen. The traffic light turned red. Of course the two mice in the box couldn't see that. The bread truck had been going pretty fast, and the driver had to step on the brakes pretty hard to stop in time. The truck stopped with a jerk, and the car just behind it stopped with a jerk too. But it didn't stop fast enough. Bang! It bumped into the bread truck, and all the boxes went crash, rattlety bang, all over the road.

The driver of the bread truck jumped down and ran to the back, but not fast enough to see two frightened mice scuttle out of one of the boxes and race to the sidewalk.

The truck driver and the car driver stood in the middle

of the road and argued about whose fault it was. The truck driver said the car driver didn't know how to drive and had no right to bump into him. The car driver said the truck driver should not have stopped so suddenly and should have put his hand out.

All the other cars and trucks began tooting their horns at the two, to make them get out of the way and not hold up traffic. Then the policeman came and blew his whistle. Then some boys came and picked up one of the boxes and ran off with it and the truck driver began to shout.

There was such a noise that Squeaker and Saltina, sitting in the shadow of a building, were amazed.

"I never heard anything like it," said Saltina.

"Neither did I," said Squeaker. "Anyway, we're all right. Thank goodness we got out of that box. But where shall we go now?"

"I don't know," said Saltina. "Let's just walk along and see where we get to."

So they went cautiously along in the shadow of the buildings. When they saw people coming they sat very still. They didn't want to be stepped on by one of those big feet. When the big feet had gone past, they scuttled along again. At last they came to a corner. Cars and trucks were going past, making a great noise. Squeaker and Saltina sat on the curb looking.

31

"My, what a lot goes on out here!" said Saltina. "My mother never told me about all this."

"Neither did mine," said Squeaker. "I used to think a mouse had to stay in his hole all day, and only come out at night when it was quiet and dark. This is much more interesting."

"Yes, isn't it?" said Saltina. "I wonder what makes it so bright out here." She looked up at the sky, where the sun was shining.

"Look at that!" she said. "That's a big light they have up there. I guess that's why it's so bright."

"Isn't it quiet all of a sudden?" said Squeaker. The traffic had stopped for a red light and all the cars stood waiting.

A lady pushing a carriage, and a little boy with a tricycle, were just crossing the street.

"Let's go behind them," said Saltina. "See, all those big things have stopped." So they started across the street.

The lady pushed the baby carriage with one hand. With the other hand she held on to the handle of the tricycle.

"Come along now," she said to the little boy. "Hurry, before the light changes."

Just then the little boy looked back and saw the two mice hurrying along behind him.

"Oh!" he screamed happily. "Look, Mama! There are two mice behind us."

"Mercy!" his mother exclaimed. "Well, hurry up. I don't want mice coming to the park with us."

But the boy wouldn't hurry. He just kept looking back at the mice. Just then the light changed again, and the cars started to toot their horns. The lady began to run, pushing the carriage and pulling the tricycle. The little boy began to yell, "Oh, the mice! They'll get run over!"

Squeaker and Saltina were frightened by all the noise. They scampered across right under the baby carriage.

The lady kept saying, "Oh, dear! Get away, you mice!" And the noise woke up the baby, who began to scream.

At last Squeaker and Saltina got to the other side. They ran in between two gateposts and sank down under a bush to rest. They were worn out.

CHAPTER 5

A New Home

"I CAN'T understand why those creatures all make so much noise," said Saltina after she had rested for a while under the bush.

"Neither can I," said Squeaker. "But it's nice and quiet in here, at any rate."

"It smells nice," said Saltina. "What is this green stuff all around?"

"I don't know," said Squeaker. "And what is this thing near us, with all the brown sticks coming out of the floor and green things stuck on at the top?"

"Silly!" said a voice over their heads. "That's grass you're sitting on, and that's a bush over your heads. Don't you know anything?"

"Who's that talking?" said Saltina, looking up.

On a branch of the bush sat a little brown bird.

"Who are you?" Squeaker asked.

"I'm Brownie," said the bird.

"Well, but *what* are you?" said Squeaker.

"My goodness, I'm a sparrow," said Brownie. "I should think anybody could see that. A bird. Have you never seen a bird?"

"Well, no," said Squeaker. "We've always lived in a grocery store."

"What's that?" Brownie asked.

"You see?" said Squeaker. "You don't know what a grocery store is. Nobody knows everything. So don't be so uppity."

The sparrow came down from the branch and perched on a stone, and the mice told him all their adventures.

"We don't know where to live," said Squeaker.

"Why don't you live here?" Brownie said. "It's nice here. I find it very comfortable."

"What is this place?" Saltina asked. "Can anybody live here?"

"It's the park," said Brownie. "And of course you can live here. It's big enough for everybody."

"But where could we stay?"

"Well, you could live in a tree," said Brownie. "I do. I don't think there are any more places in my tree, though. There are too many squirrels. The squirrels think they own the tree. But we could find another tree."

"What's a tree?" Squeaker interrupted.

35

"My goodness!" Brownie began impatiently. But then he remembered that nobody knows everything. "That's a tree over there," he said. "That great big thing, with all the leaves on top."

"But that's so high," said Saltina. "We wouldn't want to go up so high. We've always lived in a hole under the floor."

"Well," said the sparrow, "there's a mole who lives in a hole in the ground. I should think that would be awfully damp. I tell you what. You stay here while I go and ask my wife. She may know a good place. And in the meantime you'd better get up out of that damp grass. Sit on a rock, or up in a bush or a tree."

"But we don't want to climb up so high, I told you," said Saltina.

"Oh, very well, then sit over there on that big rock," said Brownie, and he flew away.

Squeaker and Saltina sat on the rock in the sunshine and waited. They were getting very sleepy, and were beginning to doze.

Suddenly, as they sat dozing in the warm sun, there was a great whirring, flapping noise. The two little mice opened their eyes. All around them on the rock were birds. They were bigger than the sparrow, and they were gray, and white, and purple. They made noises to each other. "Coo!

Coo!" they said, as they walked up and down.

The mice felt so small among these big creatures that they squeaked with fright.

"Eek!" said Saltina.

"Who are you?" one big bird asked, puffing out its feathers and looking down at Saltina. "And what are you doing on our rock?" And it walked away without even waiting for an answer.

Pretty soon another big bird puffed along and looked down over its feathers at Squeaker.

"Who are you?" it asked, and walked away without waiting for an answer.

The two mice scrambled down off the rock to be out of the way of the birds.

"What kind of creatures are those?" Saltina wondered.

"I think they're silly," said Squeaker.

As they sat in the grass, watching, an old lady came along with a paper bag in her hand. She reached into the bag and began to scatter bits of bread. The big birds walked about picking up the bread and making their funny noises: "Coo! Coo!"

Then a little boy came along. He watched the lady and the birds for a while. Suddenly he gave a loud shout and dashed right in among the birds. They all flapped their wings and flew up in the air in a big circle, and landed in a ne tree, and there they sat, perched on the branches.

"You naughty boy!" said the old lady. "Why did you frighten the pretty pigeons? You ought to be ashamed."

Just then Brownie came back.

"Peep!" he said. "Where are you, mice? I thought I told you to sit on the rock and wait for me."

"We did," said Squeaker. "But some big birds came and asked us what we were doing there, so we thought we'd better hide."

Brownie laughed a chirping little laugh. "Oh!" he said. "Those were pigeons. They wouldn't hurt you. Of course, they might step on you. They're a little stupid. But they wouldn't mean it."

He hopped about on the rock. "We'd better look around," he said. "Somebody always feeds them. It's a good idea to watch when they all come down. You get lots of crumbs that way. See here!" He pecked at a crust of bread. "Here's a good piece. You can have it if you like."

Squeaker and Saltina were quite hungry. They were glad to nibble at the crust while Brownie hopped away to look for crumbs.

When they had finished the crust, Brownie said, "Now come with me. I've found a house for you. It's right at the foot of my tree, so we'll be neighbors."

He flew a little way, and waited for the mice to catch up.

38

Then he flew some more, and waited again. At last th[e]
reached a big forked tree.

"Here you are," said Brownie proudly. Stuck in the fork
of the tree, close to the ground, was an old felt hat. Somebody had lost it in the park. Somebody else had stuck it into
the fork of the tree and there it was.

Brownie cocked his little head on one side and looked at
the mice with his bright eyes to see if they were pleased.

"I think that old hat would make a good house for you,"
he said. "It's warm and snug, and you'd be sheltered from
the rain."

Squeaker and Saltina ran up into the hat. Then Saltina
put her head out and squeaked: "It's wonderful! Thank
you, Brownie. I just love it."

Brownie flew up and perched on the brim of the hat.
"Oh, well, it isn't anything much. If we'd been expecting
you, we might have done better. But perhaps it will do.
Now, if there is anything you need, just squeak, and my wife
or I will come down. We live right up at the end of that
branch overhead."

"I wish you'd both come and see us," said Saltina.

"We can't both get away at once," said Brownie. "One
of us has to sit on the eggs. But we'll see you soon." And he
flew away.

Squeaker and Saltina sat down in the bottom of their

w home. It was warm and soft.

"This is quite nice," said Squeaker.

"Let's take a nap," said Saltina.

So they settled down in the hat and went to sleep. They were so tired that they didn't wake up until the next morning, when they heard a voice chirping, "Peep! Peep! Time for breakfast."

The two mice sleepily crawled out on the hat brim. There was a little brown bird.

"I'm Mrs. Brownie," she said. "My goodness, how late you people sleep! I was afraid you'd be hungry."

"We don't usually sleep at night at all," Squeaker said. "We go to bed when it gets light. But we were pretty tired last night."

"Hm, that's funny," said Mrs. Brownie. "As far as I know, most people sleep at night. But come on, I'll show you where we get our breakfast."

She flew slowly ahead of them, leading the way to a wide green meadow. On the edge of the grass was a bench, and on the bench sat an old man. He put his hands in his pockets and pulled out crumbs. He held the crumbs in his hands, and pigeons came down from the trees. They perched on his fingers and ate out of his hands. They sat on his hat and his shoulders and waited for more. One bird even hopped down on the bench and pecked at his pocket. Then the man threw a handful of crumbs on the grass and the pigeons all flew down and ate them.

Mrs. Brownie went to get her share too, and the mice stayed in the shadow of a bush. Soon a big crumb fell near them.

"Quick! Get it!" said Saltina, giving Squeaker a push. He darted out, but suddenly a furry gray animal with a bushy tail ran ahead of him and seized the bread.

Squeaker ran back to Saltina.

"Did you see that?" he asked.

"I did," said Saltina. "What animal is that, do you suppose? Why didn't you take the bread away from it?"

"I don't know what it is," said Squeaker, "and anyway, it's too big for me. Let's ask Mrs. Brownie."

"Oh, that old Mrs. Squirrel," said Mrs. Brownie. "She has no manners. She lives in our tree, and those two babies of hers cry all the time. We all wish she'd move. But we can't do anything about it. Now look, there's a nice piece. You go and get it."

Squeaker and Saltina managed to get a good breakfast in spite of Mrs. Squirrel. They were surprised that any animal should be so rude.

"I think mice have better manners," said Saltina.

"So do I," said Squeaker. "I wouldn't think of snatching a piece of bread from under her nose."

When the old man had given out all the bread he had, he folded his paper bag, put it in his pocket, and went to sleep in the sun.

The pigeons flew up to a tree and roosted on the branches. Mrs. Brownie flew back to her nest, and the mice scampered back to their hat.

"This is really a very nice place to live," said Saltina as she sat looking out. "There's always something to see, and plenty of room for all."

"Yes, and we don't have to sit in a stuffy little hole all day," said Squeaker. "Wouldn't our families be surprised to see us!"

CHAPTER 6

Neighbors

LIFE was very nice in the park. The days were warm and sunny. The two mice decided it was pleasanter to sleep in the hat at night, when it was cool outside, and come out in the daytime to see the sights. And there was sure to be something to eat in the daytime. People were always feeding the pigeons and the squirrels, and a mouse could easily find enough to eat.

"This is very different from the grocery store," said Squeaker. "The man there was always sweeping up the crumbs, and here people throw them on the ground."

One day a little girl came with her doll carriage and sat down under their tree. She pushed the carriage back and forth and sang a song.

"What's she doing that for?" Squeaker asked.

"I don't know," said Saltina. "Let's wait and see."

The little girl sang until she thought her doll was asleep. Then she straightened the covers on the carriage, and

44

began to walk around. She took a cookie out of her pocket and nibbled it. Suddenly she noticed the old hat stuck in the fork of the tree.

"I wonder who lost that," she said, bending down to look into it.

The two mice sat perfectly still inside the hat. It was the first time any human being had noticed their hiding place. The little girl peered in. She saw two pairs of frightened little eyes staring out at her.

"Why, somebody's living in it!" she exclaimed. "Two mice. What sweet little things!" And she broke off a bit of her cookie and put it on the hat brim. Then she went away and sat on the grass.

Squeaker and Saltina sat quietly. Nothing happened. At last Squeaker whispered, "Shall we take it?"

"All right," said Saltina. Squeaker grabbed the cookie and darted back into the hat.

The little girl had been watching them. "Oh, they took it!" she cried.

Every day after that she came with her doll carriage and left a bit of cookie on the edge of the hat. It made a nice dessert for the mice after their breakfast of crumbs. They looked forward to it. They felt that the little girl was their friend.

"I wish we could do something for her," said Saltina one day. "She is much nicer than any other people I have ever met."

"I think so too," said Squeaker. "Let's ask Mrs. Brownie."

So the next time they saw Mrs. Brownie they asked her.

Mrs. Brownie perched on a twig and put her head on one side and thought. "Well," she said at last, "I should think she would like it if you gave her baby something."

"Her baby!" said Saltina. "What baby?"

"Why, that thing she sings to," said Mrs. Brownie. "That's her baby. In that box that she pushes."

"But there's nothing alive in there," said Squeaker. "We've looked and listened, and it never makes a noise or moves. How can it be a baby?"

"Well, I think it's a baby, all the same," said Mrs. Brownie. "Why don't you find a nice fat worm and drop it into the box?"

"How could we get a worm?" Squeaker asked.

"I'll do it for you," Mrs. Brownie offered.

"No," said Saltina. "Thank you all the same, but we want to do something ourselves."

Old Mrs. Squirrel, on her way home, heard them talking.

"Talk, talk, talk," she said rudely. "What a lot of chatterers! It's no wonder my children can't sleep." And she ran up the tree to her nest.

Mrs. Brownie was very angry. She puffed out her little feathers.

"She makes me so angry I'd like to peck her," she said. "Some day I may do it. Talk, indeed! Those children of hers are the worst babies I've ever known. Crying all day and all night. It's my belief she doesn't give them enough to eat."

Mrs. Squirrel was indeed an unpleasant neighbor. Her children were always making a noise, but she always complained if anybody else made a noise. She was always snatching the best bits of food. She seemed to think the park belonged to her. The pigeons might have given her a peck once in a while, but they were so fat and stuffy that they just didn't bother. They would waddle past her and say, "Coo! Who are you?" but that was all.

One day Squeaker, sitting in the grass at the foot of the tree, saw a tiny creature, no bigger than his own foot, go past him. It climbed up one blade of grass and down another. Behind it came another little creature, and behind that another. There was a line of them, all going the same way.

"Who are you, and where are you going?" he called out.

"You talk just like the pigeons," said one of them, marching along. "Who are you, indeed!"

"But I want to know," said Squeaker.

"We're ants," said the little thing. "We're going for some dinner."

"What dinner?" Squeaker asked.

"I don't know," said the ant. "I'm just following in line. I'll find out when I get there."

"When you get where?"

"My goodness!" said the ant impatiently. "When I get to where the dinner is. Some of the ants came and reported that there was a big heap of food a couple of miles away, and we're going to get it. See over there. Some of them are coming back with their loads."

Squeaker looked. A little farther off was another line of ants going in the other direction. Each of them had a tiny crumb of something white in its jaws. They all climbed over the blades of grass and over the stones, holding their crumbs in their jaws.

"Could I go with you?" Squeaker asked.

"I don't see how I could stop you," said the ant. So Squeaker called Saltina and they set out. They went much faster than the ants and soon they came to the head of the line. There they saw the treasure. It was a cheese sandwich which somebody had dropped. Each ant climbed up on the bread, tore off a very small crumb, climbed down and started home.

Squeaker nibbled a bit of the bread. Then he nibbled a bit of the cheese.

"This is very good," he said to the ants. "Do you mind if we have some?"

"Not at all," said the ants. "There is plenty for all. Don't take more than your share."

It was a long time since the mice had had cheese. They were enjoying their feast when suddenly a furry creature with a bushy tail ran up, snatched the sandwich in its teeth, and ran away.

"What happened?" the ants asked each other. They ran about touching each other with their little feelers. "Where did it go?"

"We don't know," they said. "It is gone. Everybody go home again. The exploring ants will go out and look for

more." And they all began climbing back toward their home.

Squeaker and Saltina ran back to their tree. They looked up. There was Mrs. Squirrel sitting in the doorway of her house.

Saltina shouted up at her: "Why did you go off with that bread and cheese? It wasn't yours."

"Just as much mine as anybody else's," Mrs. Squirrel retorted. "I have two hungry children to feed."

"Come along, my dear," said Squeaker. "There's no use arguing with her. Look, there's the little girl with her baby. Let's get into our house."

They climbed quickly into their hat and sat watching the little girl. She had taken the doll out of the carriage and was undressing it.

"It's too hot for all those clothes," she said, laying the doll's sweater and cap on the ground. "There, you'll feel better now." And she bent over the carriage and began to rock it.

Suddenly Squeaker said, "Look, Saltina, look there!" Saltina looked. Mrs. Squirrel had come down the tree and whisked across the grass. She had seized the doll's little cap in her teeth.

"Oh! She's going to take it!" said Saltina. "No! I won't let her!" And she got so angry that she squeaked at the top

of her voice. "Eek! Eek! You put that down, Mrs. Squirrel. It's not yours. You leave that alone!"

She made so much noise that the little girl heard her and turned around. "Why, you naughty squirrel!" she said. And she ran after Mrs. Squirrel, who dropped the cap and whisked up the tree.

"Well, thank you, Mrs. Mouse, for saving my baby's cap," she said. "I wonder what she wanted it for."

Mrs. Squirrel sat on a branch and scolded. "I wanted it for my nest," she chattered. "It would have made a nice soft bed for my babies. I don't see why that mouse couldn't attend to her own affairs."

Squeaker and Saltina sat in their hat, trembling with anger. Pretty soon Brownie flew down and sat on the hat brim.

He was chirping with laughter. "That was a good joke on Mrs. Squirrel," he chuckled. "She's so angry she doesn't know what to do. That certainly was a good joke." And he flew away, still laughing.

CHAPTER 7

The Sparrow Babies

EVERY day the two mice were visited by their friend Brownie, or by Mrs. Brownie. The sparrows couldn't both come at once, because somebody had to sit on the eggs. If the eggs weren't kept warm all the time, they wouldn't hatch.

"It will be nice when those eggs hatch," said Squeaker. "I'm not sure I know what that means, but it will be nice anyway. Then they can both come and see us."

"My mother never told me about eggs hatching," said Saltina. "I don't think any of us were hatched, and I'm sure my mother never sat on us, except by accident."

Suddenly, one morning, they were awakened by a great noise. Peep! Peep! Chirp! Chirp! Mr. and Mrs. Brownie were flying about excitedly.

"Wake up!" Brownie cried. "Wake up! News! The most wonderful news!"

"What is it?" Squeaker asked, putting his head out sleep-

ily. "Have you found something extra good for breakfast?"

"Breakfast!" chirped Mrs. Brownie. "No, indeed! Something much more important! They've hatched. They've hatched at last."

"Oh! That is lovely," said Saltina. "What do they look like?"

"They're beautiful!" said Mrs. Brownie. "Four of them, and the sweetest little things you ever saw. And such good loud voices. And such nice beaks. I only wish you could see them. What a pity you can't fly!" And she fluttered about excitedly.

"Will you be able to bring them down to see us?" Saltina asked. "I'd love to see them. What color are their feathers?"

"Oh, they haven't any feathers yet," said Mrs. Brownie. "And they can't fly. I guess you'll have to wait till they learn to fly. Well, good-bye, I must be going." And she flew back to the nest.

Squeaker said to Brownie: "Now that they're hatched,

I suppose you and Mrs. Brownie will be able to visit us once in a while."

"No, indeed, thank you all the same," said Brownie. "We'll be very busy now for a while. We have to feed them, you know." And he flew away too.

Squeaker and Saltina sat and looked at each other. They were puzzled. They had been waiting all this time for the eggs to hatch, and now the two birds were going to be busier than ever.

And the sparrows were indeed busy. Squeaker and Saltina hardly ever saw them. They might meet them for a few minutes at the feeding place, where the old man was scattering his crumbs. Or they might see them flying overhead and call to them.

But all day the two birds were flying back and forth, carrying worms or bugs or bits of bread in their beaks for the hungry babies. And when the babies weren't being fed, they were crying with hunger. It seemed as if they just had to eat all the time.

Old Mrs. Squirrel complained about the noise they made.

"Peeping and screeching all day long," she grumbled. "Those sparrows certainly don't know how to bring up children. I never heard such a racket."

Mrs. Sparrow tossed her head at that. "Well, I must say," she retorted, "your two babies make a great deal more noise than our four. And we've put up with it for a long time, though many of us wish you would train them to be a little quieter. Everybody knows that babies cry when they're hungry, but at least *we* don't go off gallivanting for hours at a time and let them cry."

"Gallivanting indeed!" Mrs. Squirrel snapped. "You know perfectly well that I'm busy storing up acorns for the winter. What do *you* do, may I ask, to see that your children have something to eat in the winter?"

Mrs. Brownie fluttered her wings, jumped up and down on the branch, and said, "We get along, thank you. We don't need so much to eat in the winter, and there are always seeds to be found, and people with bags of crumbs. And now, I can't stand here arguing all day. I have my work to do."

And she flew off, still chirping.

The two mice in the old hat looked at each other. "What is this winter they're talking about?" Squeaker asked.

"I don't know," said Saltina. "We must find out. Maybe we ought to store up some food too, though I don't think I'd know how. My mother never did it. There was always plenty to eat and I never heard any talk about winter."

"Maybe it's something that happens in the park," said Squeaker.

Something did seem to be happening to the park. Some leaves fell off the tree. The mice went to look at them. They weren't green. They were yellow and brown.

Squeaker called to Brownie, "What's the matter with these leaves?"

"Oh, nothing," said Brownie. "They always fall. I suppose winter is on the way. But *we* have nothing to worry about. Our children all have their feathers now, and we've got them to try sitting on the edge of the nest. All but the littlest one. He won't. I'll have to push him out one of these days."

"What for?" Saltina asked.

"Well, they have to learn to fly and find food before winter comes," said Brownie. "Good-bye. I'm going to give my biggest one a flying lesson. He really is very smart. He's been begging to fly." And Brownie flew away.

The nights were getting colder now. The two mice huddled close together to try to keep warm. But it was still nice and warm in the daytime when the sun shone.

The squirrel children came out of their nest now and crept along a branch and sat looking at the world and blinking in the sunlight. Then they crept back into the nest again while their mother went out to find more acorns. She would come home with her cheeks bulging with them, and stow them away, and go out for more.

The little sparrows were learning to fly. They would perch on the branch just outside the nest. Then they would flutter in a floppy way to the next branch and cling there.

"Is this right?" they would chirp to their parents. "Are we doing it right?"

"Not quite right," Brownie would say. "Look. Like this." Then he would take off and fly with his strong little wings out into the air, and sail back again in a beautiful curve.

The littlest sparrow was always afraid to try. "I don't want to," he would cry. "I like it in the nest. Why can't I stay in the nest?"

"You have to fly," his mother and father would say. "Now go ahead. You did very well last time. Just flutter your wings hard, and don't worry. The air will hold you up."

"The air doesn't look very strong," he would whimper. "Maybe I could fly around in the tree, but I couldn't possibly fly right out into the air." And he would shiver with fright.

The biggest little sparrow wasn't afraid of anything. One day he flew right out into the air after his father and came back to the branch and puffed with pride.

"Did you see me, you fraidy-cats?" he bragged. "I did that just like Father. I bet you couldn't do it."

"I bet you couldn't do it again," the others said. "Let's see you do it again."

The biggest one was tired after his brave flight, and a little bit frightened too, but he wouldn't admit it.

"All right," he said. "Here goes." And he flew right out into the air, circled around and flew to the next tree. There he sat, calling to them.

"You try it, fraidy-cats. Come on over here. I bet you can't."

"We don't want to," they chirped. "You come back here. We bet you can't get back."

Their father and mother sat on the branch and watched to see what he would do. He sat there resting.

"I think you'd better go after him," said Mrs. Brownie.

"Let him work it out himself," said Brownie. "I'm not going to pamper him."

"But he's only a baby," the mother said.

"Well, he's got to learn some time," said Brownie. "Come on, boy," he called. "Flutter your wings hard. The air will hold you up."

The young sparrow was frightened. He fluttered his wings hard, but he didn't do it quite right. The air didn't hold him up. Down, down, to the ground he sailed, turned a somersault on the grass, and landed with his feathers rumpled and his wings spread out, looking very foolish. His brothers sat in the tree laughing at him.

"Now, you stop that!" their mother scolded. "You have no right to laugh at your brother. He was very brave. Get back into the nest, all of you, and sit there while we go and get him."

And the two parents flew down to the ground and landed beside their baby.

"Oh, Mother!" he gasped. "The air didn't hold me up. How will I ever get back to the nest? Can you carry me?"

"No, we can't carry you," said his mother. "You will have to fly up. Come along now, you can't sit here. Somebody will catch you. Hurry, now."

But the young sparrow couldn't move.

"What shall we do with him?" Mrs. Brownie worried.

Just then Saltina put her head out. "Why, hello," she called. "Have you come down to see us? Do come in. And you've brought one of your babies. I wanted so much to see them."

Mrs. Brownie looked at Brownie. "Do let's go in for a few minutes," she said. "Just till he gets rested."

"All right," said Brownie. So they pushed the young sparrow along to the old hat. With much heaving and shoving they got him inside. He sat there panting.

"What a fine big boy!" said Squeaker. "How did you get him down here?"

"He flew down," said Brownie proudly. "But it will be harder to get him to fly up."

The little sparrow rested while the mice talked with Brownie and Mrs. Brownie. Then Brownie said, "Come, now, we must be going. Good-bye, friends. We'll come and see you again when our children have all learned to take care of themselves."

Then the two sparrows began to push and shove their child out of the hat.

"Go along now," said Brownie, and the little sparrow fluttered out on to the grass.

"Now watch me," said Brownie. He fluttered his wings hard, and flew a little way. "Do that," he said.

The baby fluttered and flapped along the grass.

"Harder, harder," said both parents. And they got behind him and pushed. This time he flew a little higher, and landed on the grass again.

"Now you must fly to that low branch," said Brownie.

The baby flapped and fluttered as hard as he could. This time he really went up in the air and managed to land on the lowest branch of the tree. His mother and father landed on the branch beside him. The two mice sat in the grass and looked up at them.

"Isn't it wonderful how they can do that!" Squeaker said. "Even the baby can do it."

"Now you must take off from this branch," said

63

Brownie. "But you mustn't go down again. You must work so hard with your wings that you go up. All right. Here we go."

And with his parents on either side of him, coaxing and teaching him, he flapped so hard that he really did fly up to the next higher branch. At last they got up to the nest. He sat there for quite a while, puffing and gasping, his beak open and his wings spread out, while his brothers sat around and stared at him.

When he had finally got his breath, he began to talk to them.

"Did you see me?" he bragged. "I flew all the way down and back again. It was fun. You ought to try it. We visited some friends down there. Mice, they were, I think." And he went on telling them how smart he was, until his mother came and pecked him and told him not to talk so much, seeing how much trouble they had had getting him back to the nest.

And at last, after a few more days, all the baby birds, even the littlest, had learned to fly, and could go up, or down, or sideways, or even play tag in the air, without being at all frightened. Their parents took them on trips, and showed them where to find bugs, or worms, or crumbs, or seeds. They still came back to the nest every night, and slept under their mother's warm wings.

CHAPTER 8

Squirrel Babies

BUT one morning, while Squeaker and Saltina were sitting in the sun and getting warm after the cool night, Mr. and Mrs. Brownie flew down and perched on their hat brim.

"Hello, there," said Squeaker. "This is a nice surprise. Going out to find some breakfast?"

"Yes," said Brownie. "We thought you might go with us. We're feeling a bit lonesome."

"Lonesome?" said Saltina. "Where are the children?"

Mrs. Brownie pretended to straighten some of her wing feathers with her beak. "Well, you see," she began. "They —they've—Oh, dear, I do feel so sad!"

"They've gone," said Brownie. "They've flown away. Of course we knew they would. But we can't help feeling it at first."

"Gone away?" said Saltina. "And won't they come back?"

65

Brownie shook his little head. "No," he said in a hoarse little croak. "They can take care of themselves now. They were all good children, and they learned very fast."

"Look, dear," said Mrs. Brownie, "I think I see one of them up there on that branch."

A little brown bird on a branch cleaned his wing with his beak. Then he chirped, "Peep!" He fluttered about the empty nest for a while. Then he flew away.

"That was our littlest," said Mrs. Brownie.

"Well," Brownie sighed, "it's always like this. We raise a fine family and then they go away. But it was fun while they were little. And next year we'll have some more."

"At least that old Mrs. Squirrel won't be able to complain about the children crying any more," said Mrs. Brownie. "And next year we'd better not live so close to her."

"That reminds me," said Saltina, "I haven't seen Mrs. Squirrel for a couple of days. I was wondering if she'd moved."

"No, I don't think so," said Mrs. Brownie. "I've heard *her* babies crying every day and sometimes at night."

"Well, I'm sure their mother hasn't been home. Maybe something has happened to her."

"I don't know," said Brownie. "And I want my breakfast."

Just then they heard a whimpering, crying noise.

"What's that?" said Saltina, looking up. "Well, mercy! Look at that!"

Down the trunk of the tree, hanging on tight with their little claws, and crying softly, came Mrs. Squirrel's two babies. They looked about, blinking in the bright sunlight.

The two birds fluttered about.

"Where are you going?" Mrs. Brownie asked. "You go right back. Where's your mother?"

"We don't know," one of the babies wailed. "Mother went away and didn't come back. We're hungry." And they kept on crawling down the tree.

"But you can't come out like this," said Brownie. "You don't know how to go out alone. Have you ever been out?"

"No," said the other baby. "We've been sitting on the branch. But we're hungry."

Brownie said, "You go back up and wait, and we'll go and look for your mother."

"We can't go up," said the first baby. "We don't know how to climb up."

Saltina squeaked, "But somebody will catch you. Do you want a man to catch you? Or a boy?"

This frightened both babies so that they began to cry loudly.

"Do be quiet," said Brownie. "You'll have the park keeper over here in a minute."

"Oh, here come some boys," said Squeaker, who had been keeping watch. "Quick! Make them go up again."

"No," said Saltina, "make them come into our house. We'll hide them, if we can only keep them quiet."

The two birds pecked and pushed at the baby squirrels. Squeaker and Saltina ran out and squeaked to show them the way. After a great deal of scolding and pushing, the baby squirrels were gotten into the hat.

"I must say they're not nearly as smart as our children," said Brownie. "Remember the day our biggest fellow flew down here?"

"I do," said Squeaker. "And he was a fine, clever fellow. But I think the only way to keep these creatures quiet is to feed them. Could you birds go and find something for them to eat?"

"All right," said Brownie. "I thought we were through with that for this season. But come on, wife, let's go and see what we can find."

And they flew off. In a few minutes they were back with some bits of bread. The baby squirrels began to nibble at the bread as if they hadn't eaten for a week.

"I guess you'll have to get some more if we are to keep them quiet," said Squeaker. "And if they don't keep quiet, somebody will be sure to hear them and maybe catch us all."

"You go for food," said Brownie to his wife, "and I'll go and see if I can find a squirrel who will take care of them." And they both flew away.

Mrs. Brownie came back first with the food. After a while Brownie returned. He was very cross.

"I found three squirrels," he said, "and not one of them would come. A fine lot they are, I must say. Well, I'll go and see if I can discover what has happened to their mother."

All day the baby squirrels stayed in the hat. They took up most of the space in it, and the mice were worn out trying to keep them quiet and coaxing them to go back to their nest. But they wouldn't go. At last they fell asleep. Squeaker and Saltina, quite worn out, went to sleep too. It had been the hardest day of their lives.

"If ever *I* have any children, I assure you they will be better trained than these little nuisances," Saltina said before she closed her eyes.

Late in the afternoon, the two sparrows returned. They had not been able to find old Mrs. Squirrel.

"We've got to get home now," they said. "We're going to have a storm. A big one, it looks like."

Squeaker put his head out. It was quite dark. "Why, I thought it was night," he said.

"No, indeed," said Brownie. "See all the people running? That means it's going to rain. And hear the wind blowing. And see the trees bending, and the leaves turning over." And he and Mrs. Brownie flew up to their nest, chirping and twittering.

The wind howled in the trees. It blew a spatter of big raindrops against the old hat. The squirrel babies woke up and began to cry again.

"Oh, dear!" said Saltina. "Well, since all the people are running away, I suppose it doesn't matter if they cry. But I do wish they'd keep quiet."

"We're hungry," wailed the babies.

"Well, there's nothing to eat now," said Squeaker. "And it's going to rain, so you must wait."

"We want our mama!" the babies wailed.

The wind howled louder. The rain began to pour down. It splashed against the tree. It ran over the wet grass. Many leaves fell from the tree. Thunder rolled. Lightning flashed. The babies were frightened. Squeaker and Saltina were frightened too. They shivered inside their warm hat. It was crowded, with the little squirrels there, but they did help the mice to keep warm. The two mice snuggled closer to the crying babies.

Squeaker said, "Maybe I could tell them a story to keep them quiet."

So he began: "Once we lived in a grocery store."

"What's a grocery store?" the babies whimpered.

"Oh," said Squeaker, "it's a nice warm place where there are lots of things to eat."

"I want to go there!" the babies howled.

"Oh, dear!" said Saltina. "Now see what you've done. They're just going to cry harder."

"Well, I can't help it," Squeaker argued, and he went on

with the story. "It was nice and warm, and there was plenty to eat."

"I wouldn't mind being there now myself," said Saltina, in a shaky voice. "It makes me quite homesick to think of it. Oh, dear, I think I'm going to cry a bit myself."

"Nonsense!" said Squeaker in a loud voice, to show that he had no intention of crying. But he rubbed his front foot across his eyes before he continued. "There were lots of mice in the grocery store. But the grocery man didn't know it, because they never came out in the daytime. They slept all day, and came out of their holes at night."

"That's silly," one of the babies interrupted. "All sensible animals sleep at night. Our mother said so."

"When did she say that?" Saltina asked.

"At night, when we didn't want to sleep," said the baby.

Squeaker remarked: "I suppose all children want to stay awake when their mothers say it's time to sleep. But they always find out sooner or later that the mothers were right."

It was very late now. The wind still howled and the rain still fell. The babies were sound asleep, curled up with their little tails around each other.

Squeaker and Saltina were quite tired. But they sat whispering together.

"Do you know what I think?" Squeaker said. "I think we ought to go home."

"I think so too," said Saltina. "I don't like the weather here at all lately. At first it was nice and warm. But now it gets too cold. And then there's all this water pouring down, and lights flashing, and wind blowing."

"Yes," said Squeaker. "And this winter that they all talk of. I don't know what it is, but it sounds quite unpleasant."

"Do you think we could find our way?" Saltina asked. "You know we came here quite a long time ago, and part of the way we were in that box and couldn't see where we were going."

"We could try," said Squeaker. "And if we don't find our own grocery store, maybe we could find another. I'm sure there must be another somewhere."

"All right, let's try," said Saltina. And then they went to sleep too, snuggled up close against the squirrel babies.

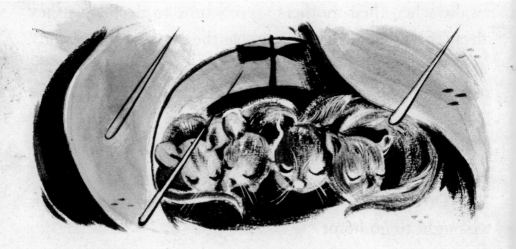

CHAPTER 9

Goodbye to the Park

WHEN Saltina and Squeaker woke up the next morning, the storm was over. The sky was blue, and the air was clear and cold. The two squirrel babies still slept.

Squeaker put his head out and shivered. "Brrr! It's cold!"

"I wonder if Mrs. Squirrel will come back today," said Saltina.

"Tweet! Tweet! Chirp!" There was Brownie, flying about overhead. He came down and pecked in the wet grass, looking for bugs.

"Hello," he said, when he saw Squeaker. "Wasn't it an awful night? How did you make out?"

"Oh, pretty well, thanks," said Squeaker. "Sh! Don't wake those young squirrels. We're glad they're still asleep."

"Good morning!" said Mrs. Brownie. "What a storm! I thought our nest would be blown away. Nice day today, but cold. I wonder if the old man will be out with his crumbs. I don't think so. He doesn't come out early when it's cold." And she fluffed up her feathers so that she looked twice as fat as she really was.

Suddenly there was the most surprising racket. Chatter, chatter, chatter! Scold, scold! Feet running up the tree, and down again.

"Well, I must say," said a voice, "this is a fine state of affairs. Where are those children? I suppose a cat has got them. Fine neighbors, I declare. Couldn't somebody take care of two helpless children? Fine state of affairs!"

It was Mrs. Squirrel. She had come back, and her children were not in the nest. She was very angry.

She ran about in the grass. When she saw Brownie, she began to scold him. "Your children are gone," she said. "I should think you might look after mine when I couldn't get home. Oh, dear! Oh, dear! What shall I do now?" she wailed.

Brownie was indignant. He was just about to tell Mrs. Squirrel what he thought of her for staying away so long, when the children woke up and began to cry.

"I hear their voices," Mrs. Squirrel cried. "Where are they? Where have you put them? Oh, my poor babies!"

"They're right in here, ma'am," said Squeaker. "They're quite all right, but rather hungry."

At the sound of their mother's voice, the babies looked out and began to crawl out of the hat.

"Oh, Mother," they cried, "we were so hungry, and you didn't come home, and we started out to look for you." They crept up to her and she began to lick them, and chatter, and scold, and cry, and say how glad she was to see them.

"Where have you been?" Mrs. Brownie asked, when she could get a word in edgewise. "We thought something terrible must have happened to you. We didn't know what to do with these children when they began climbing down the tree and wouldn't go up again. And then these mice very kindly took them in, and kept them all night, and Brownie and I fed them as well as we could. And now please explain, because we really were quite worried."

"Something terrible did happen," said Mrs. Squirrel. She sat down on the grass to catch her breath. "I thought I'd never get back. I went into a hole at the foot of a tree, where I had some acorns stored. And then a dog came and barked at me and waited for me to come out. He wouldn't go away. He sat there and sat there. And when I finally did come out, he was still there and he grabbed me by the leg. Well, I got away, but I had a very sore leg. I could hardly move. I got up in a tree, and the dog went away. And I sat in that tree—I don't know how long I sat there, wondering if the children were starving. And then that storm came. I thought I'd be drowned. So this morning I managed to get home, and I ran to the nest as fast as I could, and the children weren't there. I can tell you, I was so frightened I didn't know what to do."

"Well, you poor thing!" said Saltina. "You did have a bad time. You must be worn out."

"I am," said Mrs. Squirrel. She really did look bad. Her fur was wet and patchy. She was thin, and her eyes were dull and her tail drooped.

"And to think," she went on, "of the nasty things I said about my neighbors! To think that you took the children in and fed them and kept them warm! I hope they were good. Were you good?" she asked them.

"No, Mama," said one.

"We cried," said the other. "We couldn't help it."

"Don't you worry," said Saltina. "They were quite good, considering how frightened they were. And as for keeping them warm, they kept *us* warm last night. We were glad to have them."

But Mrs. Squirrel wouldn't be comforted. "To think of the way I fussed whenever those little sparrows made a noise! And now they've all flown away, and you had to go out and find food for my children. Oh, dear! Oh, dear! I haven't been a very good neighbor myself. But I'm going

to turn over a new leaf. I don't know how to thank you people. But maybe I'll get a chance to do something for you, some day."

"Don't worry," said Mrs. Brownie. "We were glad to help. But I think you should be getting home and taking a rest. You need it."

"Yes, I do," said Mrs. Squirrel. "Come, children. Say good-bye, and start up the tree. I'll help you."

Squeaker looked at Saltina, and Saltina looked at Squeaker. Then Squeaker said, "I think, before you start up the tree, we are the ones who should say good-bye."

"Gracious!" said Mrs. Squirrel. "Where are you going? Don't you like it here?"

"Mercy!" said Mrs. Brownie. "Are you going to move? I hope it wasn't that storm last night."

"Well, it wasn't exactly the storm," said Saltina, "though perhaps that helped us to decide. But, you know, we don't really belong here. We decided we ought to go home to our grocery store."

"We want to go too!" the little squirrels cried. "They told us about it. It's nice there. We want to go too."

"Hush, children," their mother said. "Stop interrupting."

"You mustn't think we don't like it here," said Squeaker. "We've had a lovely time. This was a wonderful house you found us, Brownie, and we've been very happy here. And we'll miss you all. We'd like to take you with us. Only we don't think you'd like it in a grocery store."

"No, I don't suppose we would," said Brownie, sadly. "But we hate to see you go."

"We'd like it," said the children. "We want to go. We don't want you to go without us." And they began to cry all over again.

"We'll come to see you again, perhaps," said Saltina to the children. "And maybe when you're grown up you can come and see us. But I don't think you will. I never heard of a squirrel in a grocery store. So go along with your mother now. And you can wave good-bye to us."

Still sniffling, the children followed their mother up the tree. "Good-bye," they called. Their mother gave them a little push and whispered to them. "Thank you for taking care of us," they called.

"Good-bye," Squeaker and Saltina called back. "Don't forget us."

"We won't," Mrs. Squirrel called. "We hope you'll come back."

Mrs. Brownie sat sadly on the edge of the old felt hat. Brownie was pretending to be very busy looking for worms in the grass.

"Brownie," said Mrs. Brownie crossly, "come out of that wet grass. You'll catch your death of cold."

Brownie came and sat beside her, and brushed his eye with his wing. Then he said, "Have you two"—sniff—"really"—sniff—"decided to go?"

"Yes, we have," said Saltina. "You know, it's getting cold, and we're not used to it. And besides, we're not so young any more. We think it's time we settled down and raised a family. So we really should go back where we belong."

"Well, if you won't change your minds," said Brownie, "we'll take you as far as the gate."

The mice hopped down and ran along the grass. The two birds flew slowly just overhead, showing them the way. When they came to the rock where the pigeons fed, they stopped for a while.

The pigeons walked slowly back and forth. They looked at the mice and said, "Who are you?" and walked on without waiting for an answer.

Squeaker said, "Remember how they frightened us when we first saw them?"

"Yes," said Saltina. "And remember how Brownie made fun of us because we didn't know anything about the park?"

At last they got to the gate.

"Well, good-bye," said Squeaker. "Thanks for everything you've done for us."

"We hate to go," said Saltina. "But we really must."

Mr. and Mrs. Brownie sat on the gatepost and waved their wings. "Good-bye," they called. "Come and see us again."

Squeaker and Saltina scurried to the curb. Trucks and cars and busses roared past. Then the light turned red and they all stopped.

"Come quickly," said Squeaker, "while they're all quiet." And they scampered across the street. Then they turned and looked back. The sparrows were still sitting side by side on the gatepost, watching them.

CHAPTER 10

Home Again

THE two little mice ran along in the shadow of the buildings, until they came to the end of a block. They waited on the curb until the traffic stopped, and then ran across the street. Then they ran another block.

"I think we ought to go in another direction," said Squeaker. So they turned a corner and ran another block, sniffing every time they came to an open door. There were a lot of shops in that block. The first one was a butcher shop.

"I don't think this smells like a grocery store," said Squeaker. And they ran on.

The next was a shoemaker's shop. It had a funny smell of leather and shoe polish. Then there was a laundry. It smelled of steam and hot, ironed clothes. The next shop smelled familiar.

"This smells like a grocery store," said Saltina, putting her nose up and wiggling her whiskers. "Let's try it."

The door was open. The two mice crept cautiously

inside. They looked around. It didn't look white and shiny. And now that they were in, it didn't smell so familiar after all. It smelled of pickles and sauerkraut.

"I don't like this one much," said Saltina. "Let's go out." And they ran out again.

Pretty soon they came to another crossing. They started across the street. Suddenly a big black cat jumped out of a doorway at them.

"Eek!" said Squeaker. "Run, Saltina. Run for your life!" They scuttled across, right through the middle of a big puddle. It was so deep that they almost had to swim. Dripping wet, they leaped up onto the curb and ran lickety-split to the nearest thing they could see to hide behind. It was a big wooden box, the kind in which bread is brought to grocery stores. They sat behind the box and panted for breath. It was a long time before they dared to peep out to see whether the cat was still there. The cat had gone away long ago. In fact, she hadn't bothered to cross the street after them, because she didn't want to get her paws wet in the puddle. At last Squeaker looked around the corner of the box.

"Come on," he said. "It's all clear. No cat."

"Wait," said Saltina.

"Wait for what?" Squeaker asked.

"Doesn't this big thing smell familiar?"

"Well, it does," said Squeaker, "but I don't know just what it can be."

"It smells of bread," said Saltina. "I think we're near home."

"That's right," said Squeaker. "I think I once climbed into a thing like this." He ran up the side of the box and looked in. "That's right. It was a box like this that we went away in." And he ran back to Saltina. "Let's see if there's a door open."

They crept along, close to the wall, till they came to the door. It was open. They crept inside. Everything was white and shiny. There were lots of shelves, with boxes and jars arranged in neat rows. There was a counter. Behind the counter was a man, cutting a wedge of cheese just like the cheese Squeaker had once nibbled in the icebox.

"And what else will you have?" he was asking the old lady who stood in front of the counter.

"That will be all," she said.

Suddenly the man stopped cutting cheese. "Well!" he shouted. "There's a mouse! Two mice! I thought I was rid of them!" And he put down his knife and began to run after the mice.

"What a pity I gave away that kitten!" he shouted as he ran. "I thought the mice were all gone!"

Squeaker and Saltina ran so fast that they seemed to be

flying. They ran to the back of the store. They ran along the wall. They found a little hole in the corner and popped down.

The grocery man mopped his face with his handkerchief and went back to his customer.

"Excuse me, ma'am," he said to the old lady.

"Such a fuss over nothing," said the old lady. "Don't you know you can't catch a mouse?"

The grocery man laughed. "Why, that's right," he said. "I guess I never thought of that. I just run after them every time I see them."

"Might as well save your breath," said the old lady. "I never run after a mouse. Throw something at them, yes, but

don't run." And she picked up her package and walked slowly out.

The grocery man looked after her. His mouth was wide open. "Now there's a sensible woman," he said.

Squeaker and Saltina, in the meantime, had popped down the mousehole. There they were, back in the nest.

Squeaker's mother woke up and opened her eyes. "Why, bless my soul!" she said. "If it isn't Squeaker come back! Where in the world have you been? And who is this?"

"This is Saltina, Mother," said Squeaker. "We've been in the park."

"What's that?" his mother demanded. "Never heard of it."

"It's a nice place," said Squeaker. "It's full of grass and trees, and birds and squirrels."

"Never heard of any of them," said his mother. "Was there plenty to eat there?"

"Yes, there was, in the daytime. Everybody slept at night there, and went out in the daytime."

"But we got homesick," said Saltina. "It got awfully cold at night, and water poured down from the sky. We thought it was time we came home."

"Well, I'm glad you did. Your mother and I looked all over for you, Saltina. We were sure you had been caught,

Squeaker. I kept telling your father so. I said, 'Squeaker *would* go out in the daytime, though I warned him.' But he said, 'Don't worry about him. He'll settle down in time.' "

"Well, he was right," said Squeaker. "We *are* going to settle down, Saltina and I."

Just then Squeaker's father woke up. "Well, well, well!" he said. "So it's Squeaker come back! What did I tell you, Mother? Didn't I always say he'd come back and settle down? Well, I certainly am glad to see you, son. Where have you been? I used to be like that myself when I was young. But I settled down. Look at me now. Well, well, well! And who is this?"

"This is Saltina," said Squeaker. "We are going to set up housekeeping."

"Glad to meet you," said his father. "Well, well, well!"

"Where are my brothers and sisters?" Squeaker asked.

"Oh, they've all grown up and found homes of their own," said his mother proudly. "We must go to visit them tonight. But I think we should all go to sleep now."

"I was wondering where my mother could be," said Saltina. "But perhaps I'd better stay here, if there's room, and find her tonight."

"Of course," said Squeaker's mother, yawning.

That evening, when the grocery man had turned out the lights and gone out and locked the door, all the mice

came out to find their suppers. Squeaker's father went first. Proudly he told everybody about his son who was so clever. He had gone all the way to the park, and lived there, and then found his way home again. All the mice crowded around Squeaker and Saltina to hear about their wonderful adventures. Squeaker had to get up on a cracker box and tell the whole story from beginning to end.

After the speech, his brothers and sisters gathered around him. They were proud to be related to him.

His oldest sister said, "Squeaker, I knew you would do great things. I always said so."

Squeaker replied, "I thought you used to tell me that a mouse should never do anything the other mice don't do."

"Well, that may be true for most mice," said his sister,

"but you were braver than the rest."

"Anyway, you were right," said Squeaker. "I see it now, because I'm older and have more sense than I used to."

Just then there was a rush and a squeak, and a fat gray mouse ran up to Saltina and began to kiss her.

"Well, Saltina!" she exclaimed. "I tried to get to you before, but I didn't want to interrupt the speech. I was so worried about you, and I'm so glad you're back."

"Hello, Mother," said Saltina. "I wondered where you were. We're glad to be back, too."

"And if you're looking for a house," said her mother, "I know of the most wonderful place. Come with me." They went off together, squeaking and laughing, to look at the house. Pretty soon Saltina came running back to find Squeaker. He was just telling a group of the older mice how they had found their way home.

"Oh, Squeaker," she said, "excuse me, but you must come and see the house Mother has found for us."

"I'm coming," said Squeaker. "Where is it?"

"Here," said Saltina. "See, the hole is right under these pipes, where nobody will ever notice it. And besides, the hot pipes will keep us warm."

"It's a good place," said Squeaker. "Very well, let's take it. You go and find something for a bed, while I hunt around and see what there is to eat. And there are several people I have to talk to." Everybody wanted to see him and speak to him, and he felt quite important.

At last the sky began to grow light, and it was time for the mice to go back to their holes.

"Come, my dear," said Squeaker to Saltina. "Let us go home. I must say it seems much more sensible to go to sleep in the daytime and get up at night."

"Yes, doesn't it?" said Saltina. "And isn't this a nice house we have found?"

At that moment a young mouse came up to them. "Excuse me, sir," he said. "I've been trying to talk to you all evening, but you've been so busy. Is it true that you used to go out in the daytime? I've been thinking of doing it."

"Ahem!" said Squeaker. "Yes, I'm afraid it is true. But I wouldn't advise you to do it. It's very dangerous. And it might make trouble for the other mice."

"How could it make trouble?" the young mouse asked.

"Well, you see," said Squeaker, "the grocery man might see you and get a cat. And the cat might catch other mice. It wouldn't be fair to them. The grocery man might even set a trap."

"What's that?" said the young mouse.

"A trap is a terrible thing," said Squeaker. "My wife's uncle was once caught in one, and they never saw him again."

Squeaker still had no idea what a trap was, but he didn't let the young mouse know that.

"No," he went on, "after all we've been through, I can tell you that home is best, and the most sensible thing you can do is take your mother's advice."

The young mouse walked away, mumbling to himself, "Well, I don't care. I'm going to try it anyway. If he did it, there's no reason why I shouldn't."

"Do you see," said Squeaker to Saltina, "how the young mice are? I've given him good advice, but I'm sure he won't take it. Well, never mind, most likely he'll settle down in time."

"Yes, I'm sure he will," said Saltina, "if he doesn't get caught."

"That's just what my mother used to say about me," said Squeaker. "Only I wouldn't believe that anybody could ever catch me. What dangerous things I used to do!"

"I used to think it would be so dull to be grown up," said Saltina. "But now we are grown up, and I think it is very nice."

"It certainly is," said Squeaker. "And what a fine grocery store this is! And how nice the neighbors are! Did you see how they all wanted to talk to me?"

"Yes, indeed," Saltina answered. "I can hardly wait till tomorrow night. There will be so much to do and so many interesting mice to meet. And we must fix up our house. It certainly is nice to be back."

She gave a little yawn. Squeaker yawned too.

"Well, we must get a good day's sleep," he said. And they both popped down their warm little hole next to the hot-water pipes.

Soon they were curled up, sound asleep.

And upstairs in his house, the grocery man was just waking up. "Can't sleep all day," he was saying. "Time to get up and go to work."